Counting On Leroy

by

Hilary Koll

and

Steve Mills

Illustrated by Sue Mason

To my Mum,
who I can always count on

Published in 2007 in Great Britain by
Barrington Stoke Ltd
18 Walker St, Edinburgh, EH3 7LP

www.barringtonstoke.co.uk

Reprinted 2009

ISBN: 978-1-84299-472-6

Printed in Great Britain by Bell & Bain Ltd

Contents

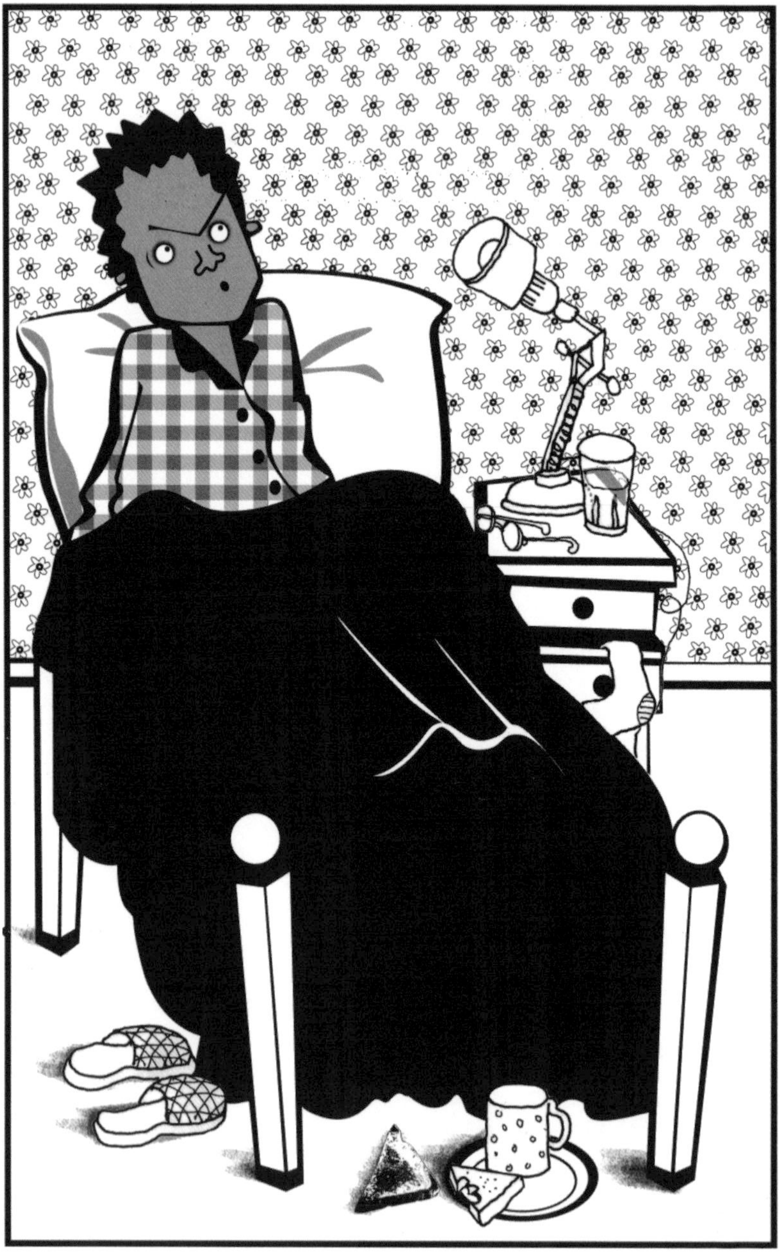

Chapter 1
In Trouble With Everyone

501, 502, 503, 504 –

"Leroy! Get up now! You're going to be late for school," shouted my mum from downstairs.

Oh, no, where was I? I tried to work it out as I got out of bed.

Which number was I up to? Was it 500? Was it a bit more? I'd forgotten. It was the same every morning. Every morning I tried to count all the flowers on the yukky wallpaper in my bedroom. And every morning, my mum shouted up to me to hurry up. So I never finished counting.

There was no time to start again. I had to get up and get ready for school.

My name is Leroy Stone. I'm 11 years and 9 months old (and 16 days and 4 hours and 41 minutes. Well, 42 now). I love counting things. I do it all the time. I don't know why, I just like it. I'm not much good at anything else but I know a lot of things about numbers.

I've got a Maths diary. Every night I write in it. Here's what I wrote on the first page:

Four is the only number word in English that has the same number of letters as the number itself.

'FOUR' has 4 letters

I like Maths facts. That's why I put them in a diary. I live at 12 Ash Road and have one cat, two hamsters and nine goldfish. I like our house number because it's the same as the total number of my pets. When I told this to my mum, she said that means if one pet dies we'll have to move house. But I think that was a joke. My favourite colour is red, then blue, then green, then yellow. That's because red has three letters, blue has four letters, green has five and yellow has six. I can't think of any colours with seven letters.

At school I'm always getting into trouble with my counting. In my English lesson yesterday my teacher asked me something but I wasn't listening. I was busy counting.

"Leroy Stone. Are you in there?" the teacher asked. "I asked you a question. Are you off in Number Land again? Well?"

"Miss, I was just ..." I started to say.

"Just what, Leroy? Tell the class."

"Nothing, Miss," I said.

"Please tell us, Leroy," said the teacher.

I took a deep breath. "Well, Miss. Those words on the board. If letter A is worth one, letter B is worth two, C is worth three and so on, then the word 'volcano' is worth 82."

A	B	C	D	E	F	G	H	I	J	K	L	M
1	2	3	4	5	6	7	8	9	10	11	12	13

N	O	P	Q	R	S	T	U	V	W	X	Y	Z
14	15	16	17	18	19	20	21	22	23	24	25	26

Some of the children giggled.

"Leroy, Leroy, Leroy. We're doing English, not Maths. Can't you think of anything but numbers? Think *English*."

"Sorry, Miss. I will," I said.

I like Miss Thomas. That's our English teacher. I don't want her to get fed up with me.

I must try to think English. But what does that mean? I said to myself.

But I couldn't stop myself thinking Maths. *What are the letters in 'Miss Thomas' worth?* I started to work it out in my head. *Mmm ... 136, that's not bad.*

"Leroy, are you still with us?" asked Miss Thomas.

"Yes, Miss," I said.

I tried to *think English* for the rest of the lesson, but still worked out that my friend Steve Watts is worth 154. That's pretty good.

In my music lesson I was counting as well. We had to listen to some music on Mrs Bell's CD player. I counted 256 music notes in the first tune. But when I told Mrs Bell she didn't seem very happy. I wish I could pull a face like that.

After Music was P.E. I got into trouble then too. I was playing football. The score was 3–3 with 30 seconds left to play. Then the ball came across to me. I was standing right in front of the goal. Everyone was yelling, "Leroy, shoot! Shoot!" but somehow I missed the ball.

The boys on my team yelled some more things then. But they didn't know there had been 23 passes since the last throw-in, and 67 since Gary had fallen over the ball.

This is what I wrote in my diary.

Some good maths facts

1) 6 is called a **perfect** number. You take all the numbers that divide into a perfect number (except for the number itself) and then you add them up. Guess what? They add up to the perfect number you started with.

It works like this. The numbers that divide into 6 are 1, 2, and 3. You leave out 6 itself. And 1 + 2 + 3 = 6.

28 is perfect too. 1, 2, 4, 7, and 14 divide into it, and 1 + 2 + 4 + 7 + 14 = 28.

King Henry III got married in 1236. The year 1236 is a perfect year because 1+2+3=6. And 1, 2, 3 and 6 all divide into it.

2) My favourite snake is an adder. Of course.

3) This is the table I made to work out which of my friends' names are worth the most. I work out how much each letter is and then I add them up. I'm going to work out my family as well.

A	B	C	D	E	F	G	H	I	J	K	L	M
1	2	3	4	5	6	7	8	9	10	11	12	13

N	O	P	Q	R	S	T	U	V	W	X	Y	Z
14	15	16	17	18	19	20	21	22	23	24	25	26

Chapter 2
Sitting Next To Lee

I don't have many friends at school.
I don't know why. People all think I'm a bit
odd. It doesn't bother me much. The boy
with the most friends is Lee. Everyone
wants to be friends with him. All the
teachers like Lee because he's very clever.
He always gets good marks. And he
collected more sponsor money for the new
I.T. centre than anyone else. He's captain of
the football team and he's a very fast

runner. But I don't like him. He makes fun of me in front of people. I think he's too bossy.

The worst thing is that our form teacher makes everyone sit in alphabetical order by our surnames, like in the register. So I sit next to Lee, because I come after Lee in the register. He's Lee **R**oystone. I'm Leroy **S**tone.

In class, Lee doesn't say much to me. Sometimes he'll ask me to move away from him. Sometimes he'll say something to me so that the rest of the class can have a laugh at me.

It's odd. He doesn't like me and I don't like him but our names sound the same. Leroy Stone and Lee Roystone. No one else has noticed that yet.

Lee started calling me 'Number Mumbler' today in the playground. Then lots of other boys started to say it too. I didn't like it so it was good when the bell went and we had to go to Science. I felt better then because I found a great fact about the human body in a science book. I wrote it in my diary.

****

1) The total length of all the blood vessels in an adult's body is about 160,000 km, which is nearly half way to the moon.

I found some other good body facts today as well.

2) The fastest swimmer in the world can swim at five miles per hour (mph). But a Tiger Shark can swim at 33mph. That's much faster than any human. And the fastest fish is a Sailfish. That can swim at 68 mph.

3) This is a good puzzle I found today.

Choose any 2-digit number that's bigger than 20. Say you choose 46.

Add the digits:
    $4 + 6 = 10$

Subtract this total from the first number:
    $46 - 10 = 36$

Now add the digits of the answer:
    $3 + 6 = 9$

This is so cool! The answer's always going to be 9. I tried it with some different 2-digit numbers and it works out every time.

So it wasn't a bad day after all.

Chapter 3
The New Headmaster

Our school headmistress, Mrs Mason, left at Christmas to go to another school. That was months ago. She was OK, but her name was only worth 112 points when you add the letters up with my chart.

We were all sitting in Assembly this morning and the new Headmaster came in. He's very tall with a big beard and a very deep voice. He said his name was

Mr Woodward, so that's better because he's worth 134.

I thought he might be OK but first he shouted at Jeremy Wood (133 points) for talking and then he shouted at Mr Simpson (136 points) for being late. And Mr Simpson's a teacher!

No one said anything after that. We didn't even move. And none of the teachers left early. I was worried because I had to cough twice but he just carried on.

He said that tomorrow he's going to tell us some important news. I don't know what it can be.

****

The names of VERY big numbers

1) A million is 1 followed by 6 zeroes, like this – 1,000,000

2) The names for other big numbers sometimes get mixed up. This is because in Britain a billion used to be 1 followed by 12 zeroes, like this – 1,000,000,000,000. But in America and some other places a billion means 1 followed by 9 zeroes, like this – 1,000,000,000. We all get mixed up because

we don't know if we mean the American billion or the British billion.

I found this table on the internet:

Name	America and France	Britain
Million	1 with 6 zeroes	1 with 6 zeroes
Billion	1 with 9 zeroes	1 with 12 zeroes
Trillion	1 with 12 zeroes	1 with 18 zeroes
Quadrillion	1 with 15 zeroes	1 with 24 zeroes
Sextillion	1 with 21 zeroes	1 with 36 zeroes
Septillion	1 with 24 zeroes	1 with 42 zeroes
Googol	1 with 100 zeroes	1 with 100 zeroes

****

3) The number of people who live in India is just over a **billion**. That's the American billion here – 1 with 9 zeroes, 1,000,000,000. India must be a very big country. In Britain there are only about 60 **million** people. There's over 16 times more people in India!

4) I like the word '**trillion**'. My mum always says 'I've told you a trillion times to clean your bedroom', but she hasn't. If it took five seconds to say it once, it would take her over a year to say it six million times, non-stop without sleep. It would take her over 150,000 years to say it a trillion times!

Chapter 4
The News

We had another assembly today and a really weird thing happened. Mr Woodward said that there was going to be a quiz, like Mastermind, between six schools. Our school had been picked. He said that each school would send one student to go in the quiz. And the best bit is that the quiz is going to be on TV!

Well, we all knew that the boy from our school would be Lee Roystone. Everyone was looking at Lee and he was smiling and giving the 'thumbs up' to the people sitting near him. Mr Woodward said, "I have talked to the teachers, and the boy who will represent our school will be ... Leroy Stone."

Everyone in the hall gasped. He'd mixed up Leroy Stone and Lee Roystone!

"Stand up, Leroy Stone," said Mr Woodward, so I stood up. Everyone was looking at me.

"Are you Leroy Stone?" asked Mr Woodward.

"Yes", I said, "but ..."

Then Lee got up to ask if Mr Woodward had mixed him and me up. Mr Woodward

shouted, "What are you doing, boy? Sit down at once!" and Lee sat down, with his mouth wide open. Everyone looked at Lee and then looked back at me. One of the teachers went over to Mr Woodward, but he just sent him away.

"Silence everyone!" Mr Woodward shouted. "Now, Leroy Stone, come here."

I looked across at Lee, who was just staring at Mr Woodward, so I walked to the front. The hall was in total silence.

Mr Woodward said, "We are very proud to have you represent our school in the Masterquiz show. I know you will do very well. Let's all clap for Mr Masterquiz!" There were just a few claps at first but then, with Mr Woodward looking round at everyone, they all joined in.

In the rest of the assembly I felt really proud. I was going to be on TV! I was sure I could answer lots of questions about Maths. After all, I was always writing loads of Maths facts in my diary and I could remember nearly all of them.

After assembly everyone was slapping me on the back and laughing, apart from Lee, who was looking very angry.

When I got home I wrote down some facts I'd found out today:

These facts are about my very favourite number. It's 7. I like 7 because –

1) Giraffes have the same number of bones in their necks as humans. How cool is that! Think how long a giraffe's neck is! And how many bones do giraffes and humans have in their necks? 7.

2) There are 7 oceans in the world.

3) There are 7 days in the week.

4) There are 7 sides to a 50p.

5) Snow White has 7 dwarfs as friends.

6) A rainbow has 7 colours – red, orange, yellow, green, blue, indigo, violet.

7) 'Rhythms' is the longest word in English that doesn't have a vowel in it. It has 7 letters.

Chapter 5
Mixed Up

The next day the boys at school were saying that it was really funny, me being on a TV quiz. Lee was still very angry. He said there wouldn't be any questions about numbers, but loads about Music or History or Geography or English. And Spelling.

That was true.

I didn't know how many musical notes there are or whether there had been a

Henry V or what the capital of Paris was. And I'd got 2 out of 10 in the last Spelling Test. I hate Spelling Tests. I'd even written "Seppling Test" at the top of the paper.

That was when I knew. The quiz was going to be awful. What if I came bottom? What if I didn't get any points at all? What would everyone say? And what would Mr Woodward say?

So I decided that I'd better find out about all the subjects I could think of. I got books from the library and I looked up things on the internet.

But there were so many subjects and so many things to look up. There was no way I could ever learn everything I needed.

And things began to get mixed up. Who was Nelson? Did he fight a battle or play for Arsenal? Did Harold get shot in the eye or did he burn someone's cakes? Or was that Captain Cook?

It was all a big puzzle. The more I tried to learn the more mixed up it all got. I was very worried.

What was going to happen when I sat in the Masterquiz chair and they asked me the questions? Would I know any of the answers? Would I know even one of them? And would everyone laugh at me? Would the man asking the questions laugh? And would my mum cry?

I tried to forget about it all by writing facts in my diary.

1) Parallel lines can be curved or straight. They just have to stay the same distance apart. Railway tracks have to stay parallel all the time or the train will come off the rails! I remember how to spell 'parallel' using the first letters of this sentence – 'Parrots And Robins All Lay Large Eggs Loudly.' I bet it's not true, but it still helps me remember how to spell it.

2) I've noticed a great pattern!

Write three numbers that come next to each other, like 2, 3 and 4

Multiply the first and the last numbers, like this – 2 x 4 = 8

Multiply the middle number by itself, like this – 3 x 3 = 9 (this is what you call a squared number in Maths)

The squared middle number is always 1 more than the two other numbers you multiplied at the beginning.

Let me show you again.

If I multiply **2 x 4** I get **8**

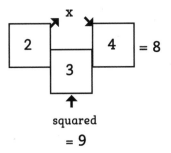

If I do **3 x 3** I get **9**

9 is one more than **8**

It works if you do the same for any three numbers that are in a row.

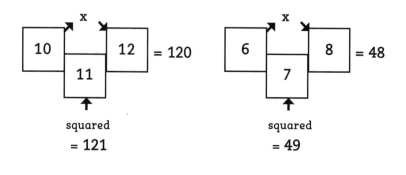

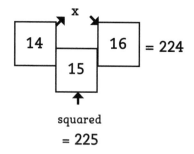

So you can work out very hard questions, like **99 × 99**, if you know this pattern. It's dead easy ... If I multiply **98 × 100** I get **9800**. **99 × 99** has to be 1 more than **9800**. So **99 × 99** must be **9801**.

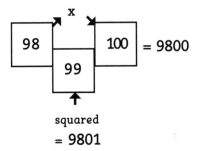

If you want to find out what the square of a number is, just multiply the numbers that go before and after it. Then add 1.

I think this is my favourite maths fact.

Chapter 6
The Day of the Quiz

I woke up and started to count the flowers on my wallpaper. I got to 107, 108 ... oh, no! Today was the day of the Masterquiz show! It was here at last. I tried to see if any bit of my body hurt a lot. Could I stay at home and miss the quiz today? No – everything was OK. Last week I'd cut my finger. I looked to see if it was still sore, but the cut was better.

"It's time to get up!" shouted my mum from downstairs. "It's the big day!"

I pulled the covers over my head and lay in the dark for a minute. But I couldn't stay there. Still nothing was hurting, so I sat up and tried to remember things I had learnt. How much rain fell each year in Canada? Who invented the Romans? Do zebras have white stripes on black or black stripes on white? Who invented the telephone, and who did he ring?

It was no good. It was all mixed up. There was nothing I could do. Today was going to be terrible.

"Leroy! Get up now! The mini-bus is coming at nine!"

A mini-bus was picking up all the people in the quiz and taking us to the TV studios.

I went downstairs into the kitchen but I didn't want any breakfast. Mum came in and said, "You can't go like that. Put your best shirt on and clean your shoes. I'll put some sandwiches in your bag. And brush your hair."

Beep, beep! I heard the mini-bus outside. My tummy felt odd. Mum waved to me as I got on. I waved back. The mini-bus was full with lots of boys and girls the same age as me and some grown-ups too. Someone was waving at me and patting an empty seat. Oh, no. It was Mr Woodward.

"Come and sit here," he said. "I thought I'd come with you because I'm so sure that you'll do well for the school. I've got something for you to read on the way." He opened his bag and pulled out a thick book called *Things to Know about Everything*.

"Thank you," I muttered. I opened the book and looked at the last page. At the bottom it said 960. There were 960 pages in it!

I shut the book and stared out of the window.

Mr Woodward said, "Shall I test you? Who invented the light bulb? What's the capital of Bulgaria? How do you spell Kenya?"

Ken who? I didn't want Mr Woodward to test me. He'd see I was hopeless.

"No, it's OK, Mr Woodward, erm ... I'll just start my lunch now," I said.

"But it's only ten past nine," said Mr Woodward, looking down at me through his big beard.

"Well, erm ... they're very thick sandwiches," I said.

"Right" he said, "anything that will help us win is fine with me. I'll just read my own book."

I put the sandwich away. I wasn't hungry at all. I looked at the houses outside as we sped past. I could hear another teacher testing someone else behind me. "Who invented the telephone?" she asked.

How could anyone know the answer to that?

"Alexander Bell, in 1876," said a small voice.

"Well done, Justin, that's right," said the teacher. "Now, spell action."

"A-c-t-i-o-n," Justin said.

"Very good, Justin." His teacher sounded proud.

I couldn't listen any more. I didn't know there were any 't's in "action". What happened to the 'sh' in the middle?

Just then a lady stood up at the front. "Hello, everyone," she said. "I'm Jennie from the BBC. Let me tell you what's going to happen today. We'll arrive at the studios in a few minutes. This afternoon there will be a practice of the show, so you'll all know what to do in the real show later. There'll be ten questions for each person. The questions'll be on different topics, like Geography, History, Music and Spelling. Have you got any questions?"

I wanted to ask if there'd be any Maths questions but I thought I'd better not.

Instead I took out my calculator. I keyed in my favourite upside-down calculator words. (By the way, they only work on a calculator.) I keyed in **3 7 6 0 0 6** and turned my calculator upside down to see what it said.

I then tried these. Remember – this won't work if you just turn the page upside down. You need a calculator.

7 7 3 4

5 5 1 4

3 5 3 3 6

5 3 7 0 4

5 7 1 0 8

5 5 0 7 6

3 7 8 8 0 8

5 5 3 7 3 0 4 5

I had just finished keying in my very best upside-down word, **5 8 0 0 8**, when the coach stopped. We were at the TV studios.

Chapter 7
The Practice Quiz

The practice quiz began at 2 o'clock. Jennie, the TV lady, put all our names into a bag. The she pulled them out in the order we'd go into the quiz. My name came out last.

The first contestant was Pauline Jones (141). She had to sit in a big black chair. All the lights went out except for a spotlight on her. It was a bit scary. She got most of the questions right, even a history one about a Prime Minister. I got even more scared.

The second contestant was called Justin Fox (138). He did even better than Pauline! David Norman (115) was next, then Deepa Ramon (61). Soon it was my turn. I was sweating as I got into the chair. It was plastic and warm and it squeaked as I sat down.

"The first topic is Geography. What is the capital of Sweden?"

"Erm ..."

"History. Who discovered America?"

"Er ..."

"Spelling. Spell the word 'because'."

"B-e-k-o-z ..."

People began to laugh. And I was so nervous I began to laugh too. I got every question wrong. Then I had to walk back to my seat next to Mr Woodward. He was looking at me in a very odd way. I thought he must know now that I wasn't Lee Roystone. I was just Leroy Stone, the Number Mumbler.

I was so nervous of what he was going to say that I just grinned at him.

He looked at me some more and then he said, "That was very clever. You got them all wrong on purpose. You know you're going to win. You'll surprise them all in the real show tonight when you get all the answers right. Don't forget, I've seen all your reports at school. I know you're going to win tonight."

I just sat there. What was I going to do? My leg hurt a bit. Maybe I'd have to have it chopped off that afternoon. Then I'd have to miss the show. But just then my leg stopped hurting.

In the end, I thought the best thing was to do the 9 times table on my fingers so as to take my mind off it all.

Hold your palms towards you.

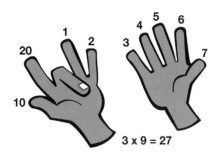

3 x 9 = 27

For 3 x 9 hold down your third finger from the left.

The fingers on the left side of the bent finger are each worth 10.

All the fingers – except for the bent one – are each worth 1. You count the fingers on the right hand too.

For 4 x 9 hold down your fourth finger and so on ... It works for all the 9 times table!

Chapter 8
The Competition

Mr Woodward and I went for something to eat in the BBC canteen. I had 5 fish fingers because 5 is a prime number and I love prime numbers! They're numbers that can't be divided by anything except themselves and 1. I had 16 chips as well. 16 isn't a prime number but it is a square number (4 x 4). Square numbers are fun too. I'm not sure how many peas I had because when I tried to sort them out they got stuck in the tomato sauce. Mr Woodward began to look at me oddly when I was moving my peas across the plate, so I had to stop counting them.

At 7 o'clock we had to all go to a room called 'Make-up' where, even if you're a boy, a lady puts stuff on your face. She said it stops your face being too shiny on the TV cameras. I was sweating so much, the make-up lady thought I was ill. She was a bit like my mum. I wanted to tell her that I didn't know any of the answers. Maybe she could put so much make-up on that I would look like someone else and then I wouldn't have to do the quiz. But she just put a bit of powder on and went away.

Then we all walked down to the TV studio again. This time it was full of people. They all clapped as we went in. The noise was very loud. A voice from a loudspeaker said, "Five minutes to go."

We all sat down in six chairs in a row. We sat in the same order as we'd sat in the practice. Pauline Jones was in a chair at one end and I was on a chair at the other end.

Suddenly the loudspeaker said, "Five, four, three, two, one, ACTION!"

The man who was going to ask the questions smiled at the cameras and said, "Good evening and welcome to this special edition of MasterQuiz. Can we have our first contestant please?"

Pauline Jones stood up and walked to the black chair. She sat down and the question man said, "And your name is ...?"

"Pauline Jones from Lowhill School."

"Your first topic is …"

Pauline got seven answers right and scored seven points.

And then it was someone else's turn. He scored six. Then Justin scored seven. I was so nervous now. I was sweating like mad. Some of the make-up had begun to run down my neck. I kept thinking how many points Lee Roystone would have scored if he'd been here and not me. How many would I score? Would I score any points at all?

The best score was nine out of ten. That was by Christopher Brookerman. I had just finished counting what he was worth (251 – wow!) when the question man said, "And our last contestant please." No one stood up. Then I knew it was me. I was the last contestant. I got up and slowly walked to the black chair. Someone – I think it was Justin – giggled as I walked past. I sat down in the chair. It squeaked again. The lights went out and a bright spotlight shone in my face.

The question man said, "And your name is ...?"

"Leroy Stone from Horton School," I muttered.

"Your first topic is Nature," said the question man. "What is a puffin?"

I didn't know. I said, "Is it a flower?"

The man said, "No, it's a bird." Some people laughed.

I could just see Mr Woodward. He wasn't laughing. I gulped and shut my eyes.

"Now a Geography question. About how many people live in India?"

I began to shake my head. Was this all a bad dream? My mum would be watching this with all her friends on telly. I wished I was there with her. But hold on! Into my mind flashed the page I'd written in my diary – the page with the facts about big numbers. Wasn't it India that had over one billion people? Did that mean I knew the answer?

I quickly said, "Just over one billion ..." but then I remembered. When America and France use the word 'billion', they mean a different number than in Britain. I said, "I mean 1 with nine zeroes after it."

"Correct."

At least I'd got one point. I looked around. Mr Woodward was smiling now.

He still thought I'd been messing about in the practice. But I knew I was going to look very silly very soon.

"Science. How many atoms in a grain of salt?"

Uh oh. I hadn't got a clue what an atom was, never mind how many were in a grain of salt. My head dropped. Was it 7? Was it 24? Was it 96? I didn't know. I thought that the best thing to do was to make everyone laugh. I'd make up a silly answer. Mr Woodward thought I was being clever when I made everyone laugh in the practice. So I thought up the most crazy answer I could ...

"Er, is it one point two trillion?" I said with a big grin on my face.

The question man stared at me. He looked shocked.

"In all the years of running this quiz, no one has ever got that question right," he said "until now!"

I didn't understand him at first, but when everyone started clapping madly, I worked out what he'd meant. My crazy answer had been right!

"About one point two trillion atoms are in a grain of salt, using the British meaning of the word trillion. Well done," the question man said.

I couldn't believe this! I'd got two points. Mr Woodward was smiling even more!

"History. In what year did King Henry III marry?"

Oh, no. I hate History ... Wait a minute, I thought. *I know this because I've got it in my diary!* I remembered that the numbers that go into 6 are 1, 2, 3 and 6 and that 1 + 2 + 3 = 6. 6 is a **perfect** number. I'd looked up things that happened in the year 1236 and I was sure it was the year of Henry III's wedding.

I said "Henry III got married in 1236. It was a perfect year."

"Correct. And thank you for telling us it was a perfect year for him. Now another Nature question. How many bones do giraffes have in their necks?"

This was another question in my diary because the answer is my favourite number!

I said, "I think the answer is seven."

"Correct again."

How weird was that! I couldn't believe it.

It went on like this until ... the question man had asked me nine questions and I'd got eight correct! Just one more question to go. Mr Woodward had a big grin on his face but I could still feel the make-up running down my neck.

"Your next topic is Spelling. Spell 'parallelogram'."

My mind went blank. What a horrible question. I was about to say I didn't know when I remembered how to spell parallel. I'd got that silly sentence in my diary. 'Parrots And Robins ...' it went. How did the rest of it go? Oh yes – Parrots And Robins All Lay Large Eggs Loudly.

Slowly I said, "P-A-R-A-L-L ..." Then I got excited and said, "... eggs loudly."

"Pardon?" said the question man. Someone laughed.

"Oh, sorry", I said. "I meant -E-L. That's P-A-R-A-L-L-E-L." I stopped. The question man had asked for **parallelogram**. I went on. "O-G-R-A-M?" I guessed.

"Correct," the question man said. "Leroy Stone, you have scored nine points. That means there is a tie for first place between Christopher Brookerman and Leroy Stone."

Wow. Was this really happening?

I felt so happy. It was all over at last. I could go home now. But then the question man said, "There will now be one last question between these two contestants to decide who the winner is. Come up to the chair, please, Christopher Brookerman."

Christopher Brookerman came forward and we both had to stand beside the chair.

The question man said, "I will ask one question. Whoever puts his hand up first will get the chance to answer it. But, if that person gets it wrong, the other person wins. Do you understand?" We both nodded.

The man said, "I'm afraid the last question is very hard indeed. I know I couldn't do it. The question is ... what is 99 times 99?"

I couldn't believe it. It was a Maths question! At last! And it was my very favourite maths fact! I shot my hand into the air.

"Leroy Stone. It is your question, but remember, if the answer is wrong, Christopher wins."

I gulped. Could I do it? There was sweat in my eyes from the hot spotlight, and some of the make-up had reached my tummy-button.

I remembered what you have to do to work out what 99 x 99 is.

First, you have to think of the numbers on both sides of 99. That's 98 and 100. 99 is in the middle. Then you have to multiply 98 x 100. That's easy. The answer's 9800. Now you know that 99 x 99 is one more than that answer. So 99 x 99 must be ...

"I'll have to hurry you," said the question man.

"The answer is 9801."

The question man looked at me. He said, "I'm sorry, that's not the right answer."

There was a gasp from the audience.

"The answer is 9799. The winner of the competition is Chris ..." Then he stopped. He looked puzzled and touched his ear. Someone was saying something to him through a microphone he had in his ear.

"We seem to have made a mistake. The answer to 99 times 99 *is* 9801. Leroy Stone is correct. So the winner of the competition is Leroy Stone!"

Mr Woodward jumped into the air and hugged a man next to him. The man looked very surprised. Everyone was cheering and shouting.

Afterwards there was a big party for everyone, with loads of cakes and crisps.

At the end, the question man came up to me. "Well done," he said. He pulled two cards from his pocket. Each card had questions on from the show. "Here's the card with all your questions. You can keep it if you like."

"Thanks, I will," I said.

The man held up the other card. "When it was your go I had two cards left. This is the other card. There are ten other questions on this card. Do you know the answers to these as well?"

I looked at them. I didn't know the answer to any of them. Not one.

"Of course," I said. I grinned.

He would never know.

AUTHOR FACT FILE
STEVE MILLS & HILARY KOLL

If you were on Mastermind, what would you like questions about? (Not Maths!)
Hilary: My favourite subject would be custard. Yes, the thick yellow stuff. When I was at school I was famous for knowing everything there was to know about custard. I have always wanted to write a book about it. Maybe I will someday.
Steve: My favourite subject would be the winning goals of my football team Stalybridge Celtic. I wouldn't have much to learn!

What would you NOT like questions about?
Hilary: Spelling. I once wrote 'seppling test' instead of 'spelling test' at school.
Steve: Cooking.

What's been the most embarrassing moment of your life?
Hilary: Writing 'seppling test'!
Steve: Mmm, now where do I start ..?

If you got mixed up with someone else for a day, who would it be and why?
Hilary: Someone with a job at Bird's Custard Factory, of course!
Steve: The England Football Manager, because there are a few things I would like to sort out.

ILLUSTRATOR FACT FILE
SUE MASON

What's your favourite fact?
In the course of a lifetime the average person will grow 2 metres of nose hair.

If you were on Mastermind, what would you like questions about?
All Chas 'n' Dave's music.

What would you NOT like questions about?
Ways to cook guts and offal.

What's been the most embarrassing moment of your life?
Running and crashing into a litter bin at Thorpe Park. I was running so hard that I knocked the bin out of its concrete stand ... and I was dressed as a wizard, too!

If you got mixed up with someone else for a day, who would it be and why?
Someone who has a pet elephant, and a hot air balloon, who lives in Hawaii, and is Bob Dylan's best friend.

Barrington Stoke would like to thank all its readers for commenting on the manuscript before publication and in particular:

Luca Abela

Tom Bassett

Alex Campbell-Shore

Nicole Dark

Ryan Degiorgio

William Fry

Theresa Gauci

Jacob Ham

Amy Hansell

Milly Hinton

Claire Lea

Dominic Lea

Tom Matthias

Kaushik Rai

Isla Reeves

Zoe Reeves

Alex Robertson

Daniel Rodgers

Ian Rodgers

Samuel Ross

Selina Ross

Tom Trow

Chloe Wilson

Become a Consultant!

Would you like to give us feedback on our titles before they are published? Contact us at the email address below – we'd love to hear from you!

info@barringtonstoke.co.uk
www.barringtonstoke.co.uk

Try another book in the "fyi" series!
Fiction with stacks of facts

Roman Britain
Assassin by Tony Bradman

Ancient Greece
Stat Man Goes Greek by Alan Durant

Surveillance
The Doomsday Watchers
by Steve Barlow and Steve Skidmore

Scottish History
Dead Man's Close
by Catherine MacPhail

All available from our website:
www.barringtonstoke.co.uk

And even more brilliant books in the "fyi" series!

Vikings
The Last Viking by Terry Deary

Boxing
The Greatest by Alan Gibbons

Rock Music
Diary of a Trainee Rock God
by Jonathan Meres

Space
Space Ace
by Eric Brown